YOMI
AND THE CURSE OF GROOTSLANG

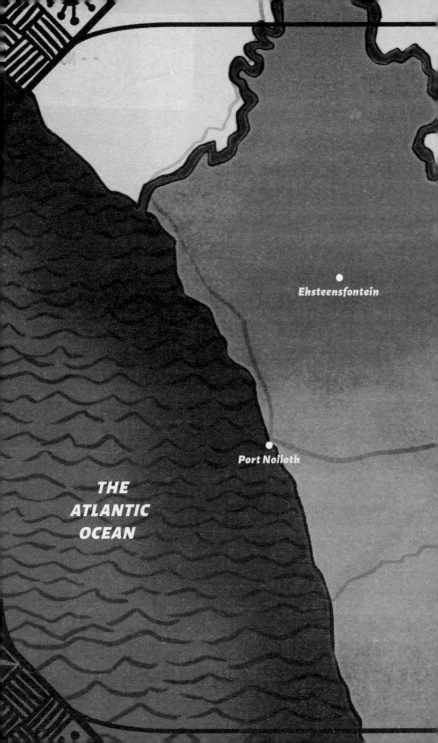

THE
ATLANTIC
OCEAN

Ehsteensfontein

Port Nolloth

NAMIBIA

● Noordoewer

● Vioolsdrif

ORANGE RIVER

SOUTH AFRICA

● Steinkopf

● Nababeep

● O'Kiep

● Springbok

AFRICA

For Yasmin, for always believing in me.
– D. T.

To Bekah and Josh my great big siblings for
always being my great big inspirations!
– A. D-B.

LITTLE TIGER
An imprint of Little Tiger Press Limited
1 Coda Studios, 189 Munster Road,
London SW6 6AW

Imported into the EEA by Penguin Random House Ireland,
Morrison Chambers, 32 Nassau Street, Dublin D02 YH68

www.littletiger.co.uk

First published in Great Britain 2024
Text copyright © Davina Tijani, 2024
Illustrations copyright © Adam Douglas-Bagley, 2024

ISBN: 978-1-78895-614-7

A CIP catalogue record for this book is available from the British Library.

Printed and bound in the UK.

MIX
Paper | Supporting
responsible forestry
FSC® C171272

The Forest Stewardship Council® (FSC®) is a global, not-for-profit organization
dedicated to the promotion of responsible forest management worldwide.
FSC® defines standards based on agreed principles for responsible forest
stewardship that are supported by environmental, social, and economic stakeholders.
To learn more, visit www.fsc.org

2 4 6 8 10 9 7 5 3 1

LiTTLE TiGER
LONDON

YOMI
AND THE CURSE OF GROOTSLANG

DAVINA TIJANI
ILLUSTRATED BY ADAM DOUGLAS-BAGLEY

CHAPTER 1

THE ELEPHANT AND THE SNAKE

Yomi was surrounded by Nkara. She stared up at their fearsome fangs, enormous tusks and feathered wings. She felt her heart rate speed up as she thought about the power of these incredible creatures.

Moving closer to the life-sized statues that filled the waiting room, Yomi marvelled at the solid gold, silver, bronze, glass, wood and even crystal used to bring the Nkara to life. Her younger brother Kayode hovered close by, looking at the Tabun rearing its claws at the onlooker. Its bright yellow eyes warned them to be on guard.

This collection of Nkara statues was the closest Yomi had got to these powerful African beasts since arriving in Springbok. The town sat within a valley surrounded by rocky mountains and copper mines. Yomi knew there were real Nkara out there for her to find but she was yet to see anything ... nothing ... zilch!

"Uncle Olu, who are we meeting again?" Yomi turned to where her uncle stood, inspecting the feather-covered body of a Pamahago. His work researching Nkara for the Sacred Beast League meant that Yomi and Kayode got to meet some fascinating people.

"An old friend of mine works here," Olu answered. "Her name is Onalenna and she is an artefact specialist with the S.B.L. She is an expert in Yinza relics."

"Yinza!" Yomi was excited. The more she saw of this amazing moon magic, the more questions she had about it.

"Didn't I promise you I would give you more answers when we got here?" Olu said with a smile.

"After everything that happened in Senegal, we definitely need those answers!" Kayode traced his fingers over the claws of the Tabun.

"So she knows how Yinza ties to the moon?" Yomi asked.

"Grandma knows *everything* about Yinza." The words were followed by a bright flash of light. Yomi turned in its direction to see a boy around her age, carrying a camera.

Yomi's eyes widened – here was a kid who knew about Yinza too!

"Sipho!" Olu greeted the boy. "It's been such a long time. Good to see you."

"It's good to see you too," Sipho answered, before turning to look at Yomi and Kayode. "*All* of you. Grandma sent me to come and get you."

Sipho grabbed Kayode's hand and took hold of Yomi's arm. He led them to another room further inside the building, where they found an older woman with thick grey braids. Behind her desk was the regal purple emblem of the S.B.L.

"Olusola Adesina." The woman broke into a big smile and opened her arms wide.

"Onalenna Magosi." Olu stepped into the hug.

3

"It's been too long! You need to come to South Africa more often," Onalenna told him.

"I do! Let me introduce you to my niece Yomi and nephew Kayode."

Yomi and Kayode shook hands with the senior S.B.L. member then Yomi cut straight to the chase. "We want to learn everything about Yinza."

Onalenna's eyes brightened. "The greatest energy in existence starts on the moon but ends up on Earth and takes many forms: weapons, moonstones, Nkara and even people."

"People!" Kayode gasped.

"How does that work?" Yomi enquired. She knew

that Nkara were connected to Yinza, but humans? She wanted to know more.

"Little is known about the descendants of the moon but they are the strongest users of Yinza. Some Nkara even worship them." Onalenna's hands became expressive as she explained.

Yomi couldn't imagine Nkara worshipping people, but then she realized they weren't exactly human. *Maybe they're like moon humans*, she thought.

"The descendants can harness Yinza for other purposes, and exactly how they do that is what the S.B.L. are trying to understand. This is where Olu comes in!"

Olu smiled. "I only just got permission to look into Yinza properly. I'm trying to figure it all out. Once I am done, you will be the first to read my report."

As the adults spoke, Yomi noticed Kayode wandering around the room. He was looking at Onalenna's Nkara ornaments and paintings of scenery from across South Africa.

"What's this?"
Kayode held up a
pencil sketch of
a Nkara that Yomi
had never seen
before.

"That is
Grootslang,
the mighty
elephant-headed
serpent. One of the
oldest Sacred Nkara,"
Onalenna answered.

"She is also an Ancient, right?" Yomi remembered
the sub-groups of Nkara from the Beast Atlas.

"Yes, that's right. The story goes," Onalenna
began, "that at the beginning of the world, many
Grootslangs roamed across Africa, harvesting
the wealth they found. Then the gods realized
how smart they were. They didn't want anyone
more intelligent than them running around so the
Grootslangs were split into two creatures – and

that's why we have elephants and snakes. However, one Grootslang survived the great splitting. She was smarter than the rest and managed to slip away into a deep cave in the Richtersveld."

"What does she eat?" Kayode asked quietly.

"Anything, but she likes elephants best."

"She must be pretty strong," Kayode pointed out.

"She's not only strong and smart, but cruel as well," Onalenna murmured.

"Cruel?" Yomi repeated. She had never heard that word used to describe a Nkara, no matter what sort of trouble it may have caused.

"But enough of that." Onalenna changed the subject. "Let's talk about Vilha."

"What's Vilha?" Yomi asked.

"Vilha is a town here in the Northern Cape," Olu answered.

"A place tied to Yinza," Onalenna added. "For hundreds of years, meteorites have landed there, but many of them were really moonstones crashing to Earth."

"And it's where we're going for your first S.B.L.

expedition – well, the outskirts at least – on the South Africa branch's yearly mission," Olu announced.

Yomi could hardly believe her luck. Finally she would be able to see some Nkara!

While the adults talked about plans, Yomi noticed Sipho had been pretty quiet but now he was murmuring into his mobile, talking animatedly in a language she recognized as Tswana. When he spotted Yomi staring, Sipho ended his call and moved closer to them.

"We've heard all about you two," he said.

"We?" said Yomi.

"How you rescued Ninki Nanka and saved the Yumboe city from the hunters!" he added.

Yomi felt a flush of pride to hear other people sharing the stories of their adventures.

"One World for All," he said.

"Are you in the S.B.L. too?" Yomi asked.

"Yes," Sipho replied. He looked at his grandma and Olu still in deep conversation. "There is more to Grootslang's story than Grandma told you, but we can't talk about it here – in front of them." Sipho stopped and called over to the adults, "Grandma, I'm going to take Yomi and Kayode outside ... to play."

"Have fun!" she answered.

"And behave," Uncle Olu warned.

"Always." Yomi grinned, following Kayode and Sipho outside.

Like the rest of Springbok, the gardens of the S.B.L. office were engulfed with spring flowers like red spider lilies and yellow pietsnots which bloomed throughout the summer. Underneath a leafless quiver tree in the middle of the gardens, Sipho stopped and looked around, making sure no one else was about.

"The town of Vilha was cursed by Grootslang," Sipho began.

"A curse?" Kayode's voice dropped.

"It is said that if people return there, it will be consumed by the earth."

"Why would Grootslang curse a town?" Yomi questioned.

"Because of 'the boy who stole'. A child once took some treasure from Grootslang. She followed him home and then started to destroy Vilha." Sipho shook his head. "That was fifty years ago."

"She destroyed a whole town?!" Yomi exclaimed.

"She would have done, but to save the boy's life, and themselves, the people of Vilha gave Grootslang the Tusk Diamond," Sipho replied.

"What's so special about the diamond?" Kayode questioned.

"It's a Yinza relic. It made the land bloom with life and wealth," Sipho answered. Yomi's ears pricked at the mention of that. "Handing it over was the only thing that satisfied Grootslang and stopped her from completely destroying the town then and there. You see, Grootslang isn't like the other Nkara. She gets gem hunger, or diamond thirst, as some people call it. Once she saw the Tusk Diamond, she had to have it. But she cursed the village, to make sure the people of Vilha could never return."

"And that's where we are going on this expedition? To the edge of a place that's been cursed!" Kayode blurted out.

"Don't worry, it will be fine. But now to the best bit – I have an invitation for you both," Sipho announced.

"From who?" Yomi and Kayode asked together.

Sipho grinned, a glint in his eye. "I can't say yet but all will be revealed at the S.B.L. meeting in Steinkopf."

CHAPTER 2
THE DIAMOND PATH

Onalenna drove them all in her seven-seater car, steering them down windy roads. Colour and smell danced together as Yomi looked out of the window at the expanding scenery. The route to Steinkopf was decked in golden flowers and fields of succulent plants.

"Look." Yomi pointed at a flying silver Zigos. The grand Nkara swept through the sky before dropping low and landing on a nearby quiver tree.

"Grandma said they can only be found here in South Africa," Kayode commented. "Are they rare?"

"There is a colony up east, so they're spotted every now and then," Onalenna explained.

"There was a family of them outside my house in

Kimberley," Sipho said. Kimberley was the capital city of the Northern Cape, where Yomi, Kayode and Olu had landed before coming to Springbok.

"Really?" Yomi said. She couldn't imagine Nkara camped near their house in London!

"Yeah, for a whole summer! I fed them and they showed me their babies when they were born," said Sipho whipping out his camera to show them some photos. "They were really cute!"

Yomi felt a flush of jealousy in her stomach. She hadn't gotten close to a Nkara since Senegal!

Steinkopf was a smaller town than Springbok, so there were fewer people walking its streets. But despite the location, Yomi knew the S.B.L. never did anything small. Their offices in the centre of town were in a big, dark, bold purple-brick structure. When the car came to a stop, Yomi bolted out before Onalenna had turned off the ignition. She was beyond ready for her first official S.B.L. meeting in South Africa!

Inside, people were waiting for them. Members of the S.B.L. immediately descended on Uncle Olu.

He hadn't been in the country for years and they were overjoyed to see him again.

"There is someone I want you to meet," Sipho announced, before he guided Yomi and Kay away from the adults.

"Who?" said Yomi.

"The other hunters," Sipho answered.

"Hunters!" Yomi knew he couldn't be talking about *Beast Hunters* – what other sort could he mean?

Sipho directed them towards a glass door that led outside to a stone-paved patio. Here they were met by a girl and a boy around Yomi's age. They were sitting at a table with a loaf of Mealie bread and a large bowl of Amasi between them, speaking in hushed tones.

"I've brought them," Sipho chimed in.

Two pairs of eyes landed on Yomi and Kayode.

"Hi," Kayode broke the silence and Yomi was happy he did. She wasn't sure what to make of these new kids.

The girl jumped out of her seat and ran to shake

their hands. "Hi, I'm Naledi."

The boy smiled, his grin wide. "And I'm Thabo, leader of the Vilha Treasure Hunters."

"Now *that* sounds like fun." Yomi grinned back, relieved.

"Is this some new group?" Kayode asked.

"It is a special new ... *secret* group," Thabo answered. Yomi understood that meant the adults didn't know about it.

"We've heard all about you. What you did in The Gambia and Senegal..." Naledi grabbed Yomi's hands. "You were both..." She searched for the right word. "Amazing!"

"Thank you." Kayode soaked up the compliment.

"Are you guys in the S.B.L. as well?" Yomi asked.

"Yes, our families are," Thabo explained.

"This is the first time we've been allowed to go on an expedition," Naledi added.

"Which brings us to the important question... Do you want to join the Vilha Treasure Hunters?" Thabo asked.

"Sure!" Yomi answered immediately. "But what treasure are you looking for?" She had a hunch it was something to do with the story Sipho had told them.

"The Tusk Diamond," Thabo answered. Yomi was right!

"Non, je ne veux pas me faire manger!" Kayode moaned under his breath that he didn't want to get eaten but Yomi nudged him quiet.

"He means yes, tell us more." Yomi encouraged

them to keep talking.

"The mission of the Vilha Treasure Hunters is to bring the diamond back to Vilha," Thabo announced.

"By bringing it back, we can bring Vilha back to life," Naledi said.

Yomi had lots of questions but she was interrupted by Olu shouting from the glass door. "There you are! Come back inside. The meeting is about to start."

There was a rush as the members entered the meeting room. They all wanted to be close to the front to see the president of the South African League address the rest of the S.B.L. Yomi sat with Kayode on her right and Thabo to her left, with the rest of the treasure hunters in the same row. She had a prime view as a man, who looked like he was in his sixties, with a silver cane, stepped forward to huge applause.

"Welcome, all," President Letang greeted them. "To members new and old." Then he plunged into the key details of the upcoming expedition.

"That's my grandad," Thabo whispered to Yomi. She took a more careful look at the man and noticed they were very similar.

"What is it like having your grandad as president?" Yomi questioned, thinking it must be exciting to have someone like that around. All the thrilling stories they'd have to share.

Thabo thought for a moment before answering. "It's great but it can be hard too. He's the most amazing person I know but people only think of me as his grandson. I want to be like you and Kayode – you've done so much. It's why I set up the Vilha Treasure Hunters."

Yomi thought about that – she was proud they had made a name for themselves. She was sure Thabo could do the same.

She listened carefully as President Letang told them about the region surrounding the Orange River and the town of Vilha. "Be careful on the road to Vilha – Nkara will be present." The thought of seeing more Nkara thrilled Yomi. "Most are pleasant, but not all. And of course, keep an eye out for Grootslang. It is extremely unlikely you will see her but we know how much she dislikes humans. In the event of an encounter, run away and run fast. Do not engage. Do not speak to her. Do not try to take photos. Just run. This is my *personal* advice to you. Grootslang is mighty and full of cunning," he explained.

The president also reminded them never to enter Vilha, to use the drones correctly and to keep a good and safe distance from the town at all costs.

The rest of his speech covered safety, being prepared and to always remember their S.B.L. training.

"How far is Vilha from here?" Yomi asked when they were able to part from the adults.

"A couple of hours," Naledi explained.

"We use drones to go through the town and check if anything has changed," said Thabo. "They will be our eyes and ears."

"We have different-sized drones that all have super-powerful technology built into them," Sipho added.

"That way we won't trigger the curse," Naledi commented.

"So the curse is real?" Kayode asked.

Thabo nodded. "Oh yeah. If we take even one step into Vilha, the town will disappear into the ground. A lot of people think the place is haunted and doomed to rot away until it becomes nothing. That will probably happen before long, regardless of if the curse is triggered or not."

"Senior League members think now is the time to collect any remaining artifacts," Naledi explained. "That's why I want to go. It's all part of our history and we need it – the good and the bad," she proudly proclaimed.

"Plus we can use the expedition to find and recover the Tusk Diamond," Thabo declared. "It's the perfect cover for us to slip away and search Grootslang's cave."

"We have gotten into *so* much trouble for sneaking off in the past!" Kayode exclaimed.

"But you also saved the day," Thabo argued.

"How do we even find her cave?" Yomi asked, thinking about the logistics.

"With this." Naledi unrolled a scroll to show an ancient-looking map. Drawn in furious sketches, it showed a section of the Northern Cape, focusing on the Richtersveld desert and the location of Grootslang's lair.

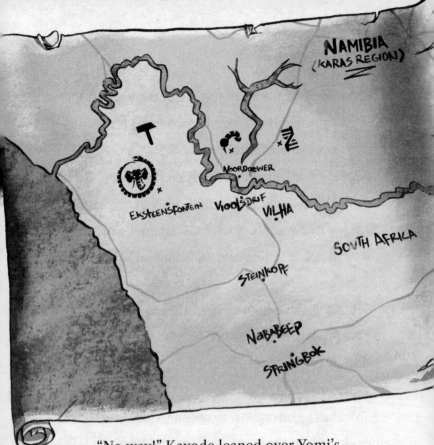

"No way!" Kayode leaned over Yomi's shoulder for a closer look. He said out loud what Yomi was thinking. "Is this real?"

"Yeah, it's real," Sipho answered.

"How did you get it?" Yomi was curious.

"I looked through the S.B.L.'s enormous archives and libraries for secrets and hidden information," Naledi explained. "The League buys information from outposts across Southern Africa, including the Helix in Namibia and the Golden Web in Madagascar. It's like stepping through the history of the world, the history of the Nkara."

Naledi's words made Yomi remember the Mansa's Stone outpost in The Gambia and all its hidden treasures. There was still so much to learn!

"It's up to us to find the Tusk Diamond!" Thabo said. "The adults will never do it."

"I can understand why not." Kayode crossed his arms.

"Come on, Kay, we need your help," Sipho pleaded.

"It's too dangerous – you're suggesting we go into Grootslang's cave and steal from her!" Kayode reasoned.

"You guys are exactly what we need," Thabo stated.

"Experts in dealing with Nkara," Naledi agreed.

Yomi made a decision. "Do you really believe that if we get the diamond back, we can restore Vilha?" she said to the group.

"Yes – and maybe even break the curse too.

I've heard my grandad talking to my parents about it before," Thabo said. "Grootslang, the Tusk Diamond and the curse – they're all connected. We have to try. If we can get the diamond back, Vilha will be reborn and people can return. My grandad will finally be able to go home."

"What do you think, Kay?" Yomi asked her brother.

"I suppose," Kayode answered, "that helping others is what the League is all about..."

Everyone nodded at his words.

"I knew you two would understand," Thabo concluded. "So you'll help us?" He put his hands out to Yomi and Kayode, who exchanged a brief look before nodding to each other.

"Yeah, we're in." Yomi grabbed his hand.

"It seems so," Kayode added less enthusiastically as he shook Thabo's hand.

"Then there is only one thing left to say," Thabo said. "Welcome to the Vilha Treasure Hunters."

CHAPTER 3
SNAKEDANCE

Nkara and adventure went hand in hand with danger, and Yomi made sure she was always prepared. She spent the evening before the expedition reading everything she could find about Grootslang in the Beast Atlas.

GROOTSLANG

Type of Nkara: Sacred
Category of Nkara: Ancient

Feared by many due to their extensive and secret knowledge, Grootslangs' existence can be traced back to the beginning of the world. Grootslangs are one of only a few known Nkara to live during the Primeval Era of Nkara, an almost lost era of Nkara history, and have survived many of the physical changes Earth has undergone over billions of years.

Having taken the strongest qualities from both snakes and elephants, Grootslangs have always been despised and revered for their power, size and intelligence. They were feared by their creators and paid the ultimate price for this. As of writing this entry, only one Grootslang is known to survive, and roams alone through the Richtersveld desert in South Africa.

This Grootslang lives deep within the desert in a cave known as the Wonder Hole, a place which is steeped in gems and jewels whose total value would be higher than some of the richest countries in the world today.

As the expedition party boarded several armoured trucks and cars to leave Steinkopf and set out into the grasslands of the Northern Cape, Yomi thought about those diamond-littered caves. Despite her curiosity, she hoped their worlds would not cross and end in disaster.

Vilha was located near the Orange River, close to the still existing and thriving town of Vioolsdrif. The expedition parked fifteen minutes' walk from Vilha, a safe distance from its borders. From there they would deploy the drones and safely explore the town.

Yomi wondered if Grootslang had ever returned to Vilha after she destroyed it. Did the Sacred Nkara feel any joy when she saw the ruined town or any regret at the devastation she had caused for its people?

Yomi stepped out of the car on to the ground, which was baked brown with lush greenery growing everywhere. There was something special about the vegetation – it glowed and sparkled in its greenness. She had read in the Beast Atlas that the

Tusk Diamond fell to Earth in its current form, travelling like a comet through space to reach the town. With its arrival, Yinza blessed Vilha making all sorts of valuable minerals grow deep underneath the ground. The curse made all of that disappear.

Yomi and Kayode grabbed a case containing Uncle Olu's tools, including his sensors and drones, which were programmed to lock on to Nkara DNA and Yinza. As they walked along the clear-cut path around Vilha, Kayode's case bounced suddenly.

"What is it, Kay?" Yomi called out.

"I hit something!" He dropped to the ground to feel around for what he had collided with.

Yomi ran over as Kayode joyfully held up a shiny red rock that glowed with the hues of a ruby, though she could tell it wasn't a gemstone.

"That's pyronite," Olu said, coming to see what his nephew had found.

"What's that?" asked Yomi.

"It's a mineral," Olu explained.

"An extremely valuable and rare mineral," Onalenna added when Kayode handed it over for her to examine. "I thought all deposits had been discovered and cleaned out."

"Good find, Kay," Uncle Olu said.

"Keep it close," Onalenna said as she handed it back to Kayode.

"I will. I want to show it to Grandma when we get back to London." Kayode stuffed it into his pocket.

From their newly assembled work site, safely outside the town's entrance, the team set up the drones and Yomi watched on as Uncle Olu and other S.B.L. members operated them. They had put up a giant screen, so everyone could see what the drones saw as they explored.

Yomi wasn't sure what to expect. Would Vilha be an abandoned site filled with ruins, or a completely barren and flattened land empty of life? When she finally saw images of it, her mouth dropped open. It was worse!

Vilha was a ghost town with sand from the Richtersveld infiltrating it in droves. Buildings had been sliced in half like they had been carved by a

chainsaw, crumbling into ruins. Even the roads and pavements had been wrecked and battered. But the destruction Grootslang had released was disjointed. One or two buildings hadn't been touched at all, almost as if the Nkara was leaving a message behind for the humans who dared return: *I can come back at any time to finish off what I started.*

Onalenna turned to the S.B.L. members who were part of the Artefact and Relic Operations unit, controlling their selected drones and the multiple arms attached to each one to look through the wreckage. "Search everywhere. President Letang said to recover everything we can. But be careful."

With her years of experience, Onalenna was leading the expedition. Thabo explained it would have been his grandfather but coming to Vilha was too much for him. "It hurts him to see his hometown like this." Thabo's voice lost its cheerful tune.

"At least you are here for him," Yomi said, which brought a smile back to his face.

"I worry about him a lot," Thabo confided in her.

Thabo's confession made Yomi even more determined to help her new friends. If getting the diamond back would break the curse, then President Letang and other Vilha people could return to their homes.

The treasure hunters split up to help the different S.B.L. teams. Naledi went off to help her dad put up a new perimeter around Vilha, to manage any local Nkara as part of the Beast Consultancy and Management unit. Sipho and his grandma steered their drone with its high-level cameras to take snaps of everything, capturing the rampage of Grootslang and its chilling aftermath on film. Thabo assisted with the recovery of lost items as he was given clearance to operate a large carrier drone. Yomi watched him as he expertly – and delicately – looked through the rubble. Despite the number of precious items he had found, he seemed disappointed.

"Are you looking for something in particular?" Yomi asked.

"Not really." Thabo carried on sweeping through the debris.

"Yomi, over here." Olu called his niece to where he was handling a much smaller drone, fitted with arms ending with hooks. He pointed to each part of it, explaining its role and how it was used to find traces of Nkara before releasing it into Vilha.

"It's a miracle that no one was hurt that day but I suspect Grootslang planned it this way," said Uncle Olu. "So everyone would live and remember what happens when a Sacred Nkara is disrespected."

As he piloted the drone, Yomi and Kayode helped their uncle document all traces of Grootslang's presence. The drone could remove the material without touching the ground, then store it in a container for them to look at when it was safely out of the town. This included pieces of torn snakeskin, a large snake scale pinned to a piece of broken brick and a scrap of what was a chip of ivory tusk.

"Is it Grootslang's?" Yomi asked once the drone had returned.

"Only one way to find out." Olu held up the scanner to the ivory piece and its Yinza sensors went crazy in response. Yomi couldn't believe she was holding the scale of an Ancient Nkara. "Let's pack it up," Olu said with a victorious grin. "We can examine it better when we get back to Steinkopf."

During their lunch break, the treasure hunters huddled together to finalize their plan.

"According to the map the cave is only a few hours away. Grootslang's cave is west of Eksteenfontein, deeper in the Richtersveld," Naledi estimated.

"A few hours away, are you sure?" Yomi wanted to be certain.

"If we get a ride. If we walk, we're talking half a day," Naledi said.

"Half a d—" Kayode shouted but Yomi covered his mouth. He quieted down after a hard look from his sister. "Half a day," he repeated more quietly. "That's too long."

"We need a faster way to get there," Yomi agreed.

"We've done enough work for today," Olu called out, bringing their conversation to an end for now. "It's time for something fun."

"Like what?" Yomi asked when he joined them.

Their uncle showed off the long bag hanging on his back. He placed it on the ground and unzipped it so they could look inside. Everyone gathered around and an explosion of smiles went off.

"Water sports!"

It was paradise on water. Water sports on the Orange River was a perfect cure for hours working underneath the blazing sun.

Kayode proved to be an excellent rower, whether it be rafting, kayaking or canoeing. He out-paddled everyone and Uncle Olu told him he should get ready for the Olympics.

"You think I could be an Olympian?"

Yomi imagined a triumphant Kayode standing on the tri-level winners' podium with a shiny medal around his neck and holding up a bouquet of flowers in the air.

"When you're old enough, of course," Olu added.

"Can't wait!" Kayode exclaimed.

Naledi was the best at sailing among the treasure hunters, having taken several courses. She sailed alone in her one-person dinghy, cutting through the water with ease. Thabo couldn't get enough of wakeboarding. Yomi watched in awe as he twisted and turned fast through the water before completing tricks taking him high into the air.

The Orange River was big enough for scuba diving and Sipho, his grandma and many others donned scuba gear and dived into the water. Of course, Sipho and Onalenna had taken their cameras, which were fitted with waterproof lenses. Sipho submerged himself into the blue to explore the silt-covered bottom and swim among the beds of reeds and weeds

to take shots of mudfish, carp, yellowfish and catfish.

"Maybe we could use the river to get there," Yomi suggested to Kayode and Naledi as they paddled out on their rafts.

"Like row part of the way there and walk the rest?" Naledi said, to which Yomi nodded.

"There aren't any crocodiles, are there?!" Kayode said nervously.

"Why are you worried about crocodiles?" Naledi asked.

"We were nearly eaten by some before a Nkara tried to destroy our boat!"

Naledi's mouth dropped open as Kayode told her the story.

Yomi listened in as Kayode and Naledi chatted, but her mind wandered. She looked out into the vastness of the riverlands and wondered where Grootslang was right now. And what she would actually do if they came face to face with the fierce Nkara.

CHAPTER 4

A NIGHT ON THE ORANGE RIVER

The light of the moon danced its way along the Orange River. Close to the water's edge, several tents had been put up. Yomi, Kayode and the other kids were all sharing a large one.

They were camping between Vilha and Vioolsdrif, a place Yomi had ventured into with Uncle Olu to grab some snacks.

It was late, around midnight, and the group were still up, talking to each other from within their sleeping bags. Kayode kept moving his feet and hitting Yomi's back. She responded by zipping him tightly in his sleeping bag so his limbs were under control. Even though they were trying to whisper and keep their voices low, it didn't stop Uncle Olu,

Onalenna and Naledi's dad taking turns to come to their tent to tell them to go to sleep, since they had an early morning start.

But how could they sleep when Naledi was telling scary stories!

"The Bulgu is the Axe Watcher of Ethiopia. His head is shaped like an axe's blade and he has four bulgy eyes that stare into your soul. The Bulgu stands at ten feet tall, and they say he can read minds." Naledi waved her hands high in the air. "Bulgu can read your feelings and knows how to get them out of you."

Yomi was blown away by Naledi's storytelling skills, her voice gentle yet vivid in the ways she conjured up the Bulgu in Yomi's mind.

"Doesn't he eat children too?" Thabo added.

Kayode moaned when Naledi confirmed this, and when Sipho suddenly grabbed his feet he yelped.

"We really need to get some sleep," Thabo said after Naledi brought her tale to its end.

Even though Yomi agreed, her mind was still buzzing with everything she'd seen so far. Grootslang's snake scale, the wrecked buildings, the ivory piece, along with the old Richtersveld maps, the story of the Vilha curse and the treasure caves they still had to find. "But we need to figure out how to get into Grootslang's cave without our families catching on, and of course, most importantly ... how not to get caught by Grootslang," Yomi stated.

Sipho yawned. "I'm tired. Can't we talk about this in the morning... I'm better at planning after breakfast."

"We're only going to be here for a few more days," Thabo declared. "We need to go deeper into the desert. But you're right, let's figure it out in the morning. Everyone needs to get some sleep."

And with that, silence finally fell in the tent.

GGGGRRRRRRRRRR!!!!!!

Yomi sat up. "What's that?" It was an angry sound.

"It's a Kaloa," Sipho explained. Yomi pictured the four-legged creature, the build of a medium-sized dog.

"Sipho is right," Thabo seconded and Yomi noticed he looked a little flustered and sweaty.

"What's wrong with you?" she questioned.

"Nothing," Thabo answered, refusing to make eye contact.

"Kaloas often pass through the area," Naledi agreed.

"Are you sure?" Kayode asked when the noise came out again, ringing closer to the tent.

"It sounds bigger," Yomi added. "Like, a thousand

times larger than a Kaloa."

The low growling turned into a solid rumbling sound and the space around the tent started to rattle and shake as if moving along to a skidding beat.

"That's not a Kaloa," said Yomi, and Sipho grabbed his camera in response from his bag.

"Not everything is photo time," Naledi said.

"Yes, it is." Sipho put on a new lens before adjusting it.

Yomi moved to the tent door and slowly unzipped the entrance.

"Yomi!" Kayode fussed.

"Shhh!" Yomi put her head out of the tent. It took a few moments for her eyes to get used to the dark. She could hear the earth cracking and crunching, the sounds of stone and rock crashing against each other. The adults were already up, talking about what could be causing the disturbance. After a few long moments of silence had passed, Yomi thought whatever it was had gone, but then she saw something in the distance. The red glint of a pair of eyes in the darkness. Staring right at her.

"Grootslang!" someone shouted at the top of their lungs.

"What!" Kayode said as the camp reacted like an exploding volcano, everyone shouting and screaming in fear.

"I warned you not to come here, humans," a voice rattled far into the night. "Now you will see my wrath." A series of exploding sounds could be heard coming from the direction of Vilha, the noise of buildings collapsing followed by a bellowing. The town was being sucked into the ground. The curse had been triggered, but by what?

"Everybody, run!" Yomi grabbed Kayode and the pair led the charge out of the tent.

Panic shattered the dark with the fierce roars of the Nkara echoing in the distance and getting closer.

"Abandon camp!" Yomi heard Olu shout. "Everyone head to the riverbank, the cars, get out of here now, before it is too late!"

"Uncle!" Yomi shouted back and she could make him out vaguely in the night.

"Yomi, take Kay and the others and run. We will find you," her uncle told her.

"What about you?" Yomi argued.

"Don't worry about me. I need to make sure everyone gets out. Go now," he instructed. "Head to the river. She doesn't like water."

"Let's do as Uncle says," Yomi said to the others, trying to stay calm. She, Kayode and the treasure hunters made a mad dash to the riverbank in their pyjamas.

The waters were still and undisturbed when they arrived.

"Where is Thabo?" Naledi cried.

Dread seized at Yomi's heart. Had they accidentally left him behind?

They all called his name and at last Thabo heaved into sight, tugging several bags behind him.

"I had to get these," he told the others. He threw the smallest bag marked with the S.B.L. logo at Sipho.

The photographer ripped the bag's outer layer, removed the package inside and pulled on a golden cable before throwing it on to the river where it grew into a giant inflatable raft.

"Grab the bags," Thabo told the others. "And everyone put on a life jacket."

Everyone did as he said. Yomi tightened Kayode's jacket to the point he complained. "It's going to be OK," she assured him.

"As long as you're with me it will be," Kay responded, and Yomi pressed her hand on his shoulder. She would keep him safe. They would keep each other safe.

Another growl from close by reached out to them and Yomi immediately pulled Kayode behind her.

"Everyone grab a paddle and get on the raft!" Thabo ordered.

The water was cooling and fresh and it splashed on Yomi's skin as she and the others battered their paddles against it. With only the moon's light to guide them, it was hard to see where they were going but they continued forward. Yet no matter how far they paddled, the eerie shrieks of what sounded like a hissing elephant followed them.

It seemed like Grootslang was everywhere but nowhere – Yomi couldn't see the Nkara or her haunting red eyes.

"I can't believe we triggered the curse," Naledi moaned. "Maybe we should have forgotten Vilha."

"But how was it even set off? We were all in bed," said Kayode.

"Whatever happened was an accident! But now the worst has happened, we can focus on putting it right," Thabo raised.

"What do you mean an accident?" Yomi questioned.

"Everybody paddle faster." Thabo ignored Yomi as he quickened his paddling.

Kayode took charge timing everyone's rowing until the team formed a tight rhythm. They cut through the waters with ease despite their shaking hands and worried murmurs. Did everyone get out of the camp safely? What would happen to Vilha now? They paddled together for what seemed like hours until the early light of the sun started to rise and take the moon's place.

With everyone struggling to keep their eyes open, they decided to try to catch some sleep, knowing they had put some distance between themselves and Grootslang. Thabo offered to keep watch while the rest of them slept but was soon snoring loudly.

Yomi kept her arm over Kayode, promising again to keep him safe. And as sleep finally caught up with her, the ominous hissing remained loud in Yomi's head, as if prepared to chase until it finally captured her.

CHAPTER 5
ONE WORLD
FOR ALL

Yomi trudged up the muddy banks of the river and quickly changed out of her pyjamas and into the official purple S.B.L. action suit that Thabo handed her. She didn't know how he'd had time to pull these supplies together so quickly during their escape from Grootslang, but she was glad he had!

"What else were you able to pack?" Kayode asked while Thabo looked through the bags.

"First-aid kit, water bottles, dried food and some of my grandad's inventions." He pulled out smaller rucksacks and started splitting the load from the boat for everyone to carry.

"Inventions?" Yomi asked.

"Grandad founded the Science Unit of the

League. He's always working on new things."

"Like what?" Yomi questioned further.

Thabo pulled out a waist bag and everyone gathered around to see what was inside. First, he held up a silver tube. "This is an expanding rope which lets out a thick cable, made of fibres my grandad developed in his lab. He won an award for it," he explained, tucking it into the side of his backpack. Thabo then held up a sphere, the same size as a tennis ball, before handing it to Sipho. "The orb," he announced proudly. "The most powerful light on Earth, it can light up the darkest parts of the globe."

"That would be *so* good for taking photos," Sipho commented.

They were all cool things and would be useful in getting them back to safety, Yomi thought as Sipho played with the orb. The next item was a thin stick, the same length as a water bottle. Yomi wondered what it was. Thabo shook the stick and it extended into an extra-long battle-ready rod. "In case we have to fight."

"I hope we don't." Kayode hugged his arms around his chest.

Yomi noticed several small spheres in the waist bag and picked them up. They were heavier than she expected. She put them to her nose and breathed in each of their scents. Lavender, cinnamon and one that reminded her of oranges.

"Those are scent globes," Thabo explained. "Press the top and they emit a strong smell. My mum smelled like an orange for days when she helped Grandad test them!"

Yomi went to return them to the bag but Thabo suggested she keep them. She tied the bag to her waist and handed a few of the scent globes to Kayode who put them in his pocket.

"How did you have time to get all of this together?" Yomi asked suspiciously.

"I thought it would be good to pack a mission kit before we even left Steinkopf," Thabo answered.

"Thabo always thinks ahead," Sipho pointed out.

Perhaps too far ahead... Yomi looked sharply at Thabo. "Thabo, did you have something to do with setting off the curse?" The question stopped everyone in their tracks.

"Of course not," he said shyly, avoiding Yomi's stare.

"Then look at me and say you didn't do anything," Yomi challenged, daring him to do so.

Thabo looked at her and the expression on his face revealed the truth.

"What happened??" Sipho cried.

"It was an accident, really. I was using the drone to see if the Tusk Diamond was anywhere.

I always suspected Grootslang might have left it in town to try to lure us there," Thabo explained. "But the drone got trapped under some loose rubble on its way out so I had to free it."

"Thabo." Naledi said his name with great disappointment.

"I took, like, one or two steps past the border. I didn't think it would trigger the curse. Especially when nothing happened straight away," Thabo replied. "But now I'm even more determined to find the Tusk and put things right."

Yomi could hear the guilt struggling against the confidence in his voice. She glanced around at Kayode and her fellow treasure hunters. None of this was part of the plan.

"So what do we do now? Where are we?" Kayode asked, looking to Yomi for an answer.

She wasn't sure. Grootslang had completely thrown them off course. The only thing she knew was that they were far from Vilha and Vioolsdrif.

Yomi watched as Naledi unrolled the map, pulled a compass out of her pocket and traced her fingers along it to confirm their exact location. "We went west down the river but we floated even further while we slept. We've actually come off the Uhabis River and crossed the border into Namibia! We are in Karas Region."

"What?" Sipho said.

"Grootslang chased us out of the country!"
Kayode looked at the golden canyons and
mountains that surrounded them.

"Then we need to get back," Thabo proclaimed.

"Let's rest for a minute before we decide our
next move," Yomi suggested and everyone nodded.
"What's the closest town?" she asked Naledi.

"Noordoewer," Naledi offered. "There's an outpost there – the Helix – where we can send a message to our families. There's also a bridge we can use to cross back into South Africa since it is directly across the border from Vioolsdrif."

"Perfect." Yomi could already see their journey play out in her head.

"Then we can head to the Richtersveld," Thabo said.

"One thing at a time," Yomi said. "Let's get back into South Africa first." She said this directly to Thabo who nodded reluctantly. She could feel his increasing desire to go after the missing diamond and break the curse but Yomi wasn't sure if that was still an option. They needed to get back to Uncle Olu and the rest of their families. Hopefully they were all safe.

"Which way to Noordoewer?" Kayode asked Naledi.

Naledi shifted on her feet and pointed. "South-east, around an hour and a half's walk."

"Fine, let's follow that plan." Thabo readjusted

his backpack. "Everyone drink water and remember our training. We are S.B.L. members," he said to the group. "Stay calm, cool and concentrate." He put his hand out, prompting everyone else to put their hand over each other's.

"One World for All," Thabo roared, lifting his hand as everyone else did the same.

"One World for All!"

CHAPTER 6
STINGER'S END

Stay calm and cool, and concentrate. Yomi repeated those words like a chant to keep herself steady on her feet and remind herself to stay alert at all times.

They were journeying through Karas Region, home to quiver trees and orange-and-yellow-hued sand dunes. There was an eerie quietness to this area and Naledi explained this was one of the places in Namibia with the lowest density of people. The Great Karas Mountains hovered in the near distance and like the rest of the region, it was home to different types of Nkara. Yomi knew that while some Nkara would be visible, others kept themselves hidden. And why shouldn't they?

This was *their* land, the treasure hunters were the trespassers. The group were moving into uncharted territory.

"Where are we now?" Yomi asked Naledi.

"We are about to enter Stinger's End." Naledi pointed to the gigantic rock formation on the map, which resembled the sharpened tip of a thorn. It was marked as a small region, as if bordered off from everywhere else.

"Is that why it's called Stinger's End?" Yomi asked.

"Not sure," Naledi said. "No one comes out here. That's another reason we haven't bumped into anyone. When I did my research on this area, there was barely anything about it in the S.B.L. records."

"And we weren't supposed to end up over here," Kayode reminded her.

"I'm so happy I brought a couple of lenses with me, so we can show the S.B.L. when we get back." Sipho had been taking photos on their journey.

As the group took steady steps into the area known as Stinger's End, the ground became a moist mixture of soil and sand. "Maybe we should have gone round," Yomi thought out loud. She feared they would sink into it. Only the rocks dotted around gave her any reassurance.

CLUCK CLUCK CLUCK CLUCKKKK

"What was that?" Kayode said as the group came to an immediate stop.

It sounded furious and Kayode soon got his answer.

A sharp yellow bulb stabbed through the sandy mixture.

"No way!" Kayode voiced all of their thoughts as the tip of the bulb continued to rise out of the ground.

The sharpened bulb became a long tail attached to a golden-brown boned creature with oversized pincers. Several more soared up to surround them.

"Roklens!" Yomi shouted as more and more sprouted into view, breaking out of the ground like angry plants. The Grand Nkara were supposed to be extinct, hunted to their end by humans who prized their giant claws. These Roklens were definitely *not* extinct.

Yomi spoke up for the group, stepping forward. "Roklens, we are so sorry for coming on to your land." The biggest one snapped its pincer in her direction, clearly not wanting to hear her apologies or excuses.

"We are *extremely* sorry," Kayode added, but this only increased the Roklens' anger as they shifted from side to side, shaking their claws aggressively.

Round yellow eyes captured Yomi and she was imprisoned by them.

"They don't seem to want to talk this out," Thabo reasoned.

"So what do we do?" Kayode croaked, pointing at the stingers, which were starting to swell in size.

"There's only one thing we can do... Sipho, now!" Thabo shouted.

While everyone had been trying to negotiate with the Roklens, Sipho had switched his camera to his most powerful lens. He put it into position, turned up the settings and FLASH!!!

Sipho's camera exploded in an overpowering glow, capturing a photo of the Roklens. The brightness was intense, even for the group, and the Roklens hissed, swinging from side to side in confusion.

Thabo unleashed the rod and smacked one large claw out of the way, creating a path to move forward.

"Run!" Yomi shouted to the others. She charged forward after Thabo, who continued to slap pincers out of the way.

"Watch out for the stingers," Kayode cried as he dodged a large one that flicked in between him and Yomi, piercing right into the ground.

The hunters dashed through the spaces around the Roklens.

The Roklens were much larger and heavier than them but not as fast or nimble. The group used this weakness to avoid the pack. The creatures made clucking sounds at them, each noise becoming more and more menacing.

Smaller pincers started reaching out from the ground to grab at them, and Yomi just managed to swerve herself and Kayode out of the way. They landed on a rock and Yomi stood up, grabbed Kayode and jumped to the one ahead of them.

"Stick to the rocks," Yomi called to the others.

"And keep moving," Kayode added.

The group stayed together, jumping from rock to rock, which proved to be easier than running on the sand.

However, the Roklens had recovered from Sipho's flash and started to encircle them once again, closing off their exit routes. When one appeared out of the ground, Yomi had to drag Thabo back with a split second to spare. Thabo was clearly panicking, despite his attempts to put on a brave stance.

"This is really not good." Kayode pressed up against Yomi. She had to agree and pressed her hand against her mouth, unsure of what to say, until a crisp citrus smell hit her nostrils hard and pushed her back into fight mode.

"Kay, the scent globes!" Yomi dug her hand into her waist bag and as the Roklens drew closer she threw a couple of spheres towards them. They emitted a blast of purplish-pink gas into the air, the smell of lavender swirling around the creatures and causing them to scream in a cry of panic and pain.

Kayode threw one behind them, and this time, a golden hue infiltrated the air. Cinnamon in all its heaviness coated the Roklens, causing them to sting themselves and each other before sinking back into their burrows deep within the ground. Their shrieks and screeches were strong on her ears and Yomi felt terrible. She never wanted to hurt a Nkara but she'd had no choice.

Determined to keep herself, her brother and her friends safe, Yomi made a tricky decision and threw another scented sphere at the remaining Roklens. At this point, they retreated, their cries painful, as if apologizing to her before sinking out of sight.

CHAPTER 7
THE HELIX

The sign to Noordoewer was battered and clawed but it showed they were around halfway to the town. Despite being happy they were on safer ground, Yomi kept thinking about the wounded Nkara, creatures she'd always wanted to protect and now had hurt. She felt like she had gone against her job as a member of the S.B.L. but she'd made a promise to protect Kayode and the rest of the group and would stick to it.

"I feel terrible about what just happened," Kayode said when the group could finally catch their breath.

"Same," Yomi said. The Roklens' hisses of fear lingered in the air even though they had long left the danger at Stinger's End.

The run-in with the Roklens had left everyone shaken. Thabo was trying to calm Sipho who was still trembling. Yomi tried to keep everyone's spirits up as Naledi led the way and kept them on track.

The group stuck to their plan to head to the Helix. From there, they would continue on back to South Africa. Yomi also hoped they could get more supplies from the outpost that would help with their ever-changing mission.

Yomi was in awe when the Helix finally came into sight. It was a building like no other. Made completely from sand, it stood alone on a low ridge. The sun beat down on the fortress's thick spiral pillars that rose from the ground, spinning round and round and round like a corkscrew.

Once inside the Helix, the treasure hunters felt like they had been transported to the Arctic – the rooms were so cold! Now they were finally out of the heat, the relief that passed through the group was overwhelming. Yomi soaked up the cool air, wishing she could take it with her.

When she looked around, Yomi was taken aback by all the different equipment on display. There were foldable power bikes and climbing gear, and a pair of special tinted glasses. She picked them up and put them on. They fitted her face like swimming goggles but had three different-coloured buttons on the rim of the left eye. Yomi pressed the first button, switching her world from normal vision into thermal colours that picked up everyone's body heat. She tried the next, which gave a greenish-hue view – night vision. The final button was an

intensifier that made everything appear sharper and clearer.

Yomi removed the specs and knew she wanted them. She watched Sipho pick out better desert clothing, masks and boots for the group, Naledi gather more sun protection and food supplies, while Thabo picked up some climbing gear and an extra large sand-proof sheet. He also suggested they each chose one of the power bikes. "We'll need them to cross the desert and we can return them later, once we've been reunited with the S.B.L."

"Do we have any money for this stuff?" Yomi asked. In The Gambia they hadn't had any money, so Kayode had traded his comics. She wasn't sure if that would work twice.

"We don't need money," Thabo assured her. "Follow me."

He guided them to the front desk, where an older woman wearing a dark gold visor was typing frantically on her laptop. She seemed lost in her work.

"Yes. How can I help you?" She stopped typing to look down at them.

"We would like to purchase all of this." Thabo gestured to their items.

"Cash or card?"

"This card." Thabo handed a card to the woman who examined it.

She raised her eyebrow. "You are with the S.B.L.?"

They all nodded.

"Have you come from Vilha? We heard that Grootslang's curse completely swallowed Vilha and

70

she destroyed the S.B.L. camp at the Orange River."

"Do you know if everyone got out safely?" Thabo asked as the group exchanged horrified looks.

The woman nodded, confirming that they had.

"Could you let them know we're OK?" Yomi asked.

"We of the Igwe outposts do not get involved in League or hunters' business but I can send them a message. Hold on a moment, I need to go to the back to process it."

When the woman disappeared, Kayode turned on the group. "I think we need to just get back to the S.B.L. and forget about the diamond."

Thabo looked devastated.

"I know you feel bad about triggering the curse and you want to fix things, but this is too dangerous. Grootslang is angry! And you know how worried our families must be. Give us one reason why we should still go looking for the Tusk Diamond."

Thabo dropped his head, before finding the courage to speak. "The boy who stole."

"What's that got to do with you?" Kayode asked.

"Thabo, you don't have to talk about it if you don't want to," Naledi said.

"No, they deserve to know the truth. The boy who stole ... was my grandad."

Yomi let out a joint gasp with Kayode. She couldn't believe the president was the reason Grootslang destroyed Vilha.

"He has never forgiven himself. That's why I want to get the diamond back and break this awful curse, especially now I've made things worse. I need to fix it. This is so important to my family, especially my grandad. Ever since that day, he vowed to make up for his mistake, which is why he joined the S.B.L."

Nobody knew what to say.

Thabo continued, breaking the silence. "I love my granddad more than anything and I'm going to break that curse no matter what ... even if I have to go alone." He turned to Naledi and Sipho. "Take Yomi and Kay back to Vioolsdrif. Go back t—"

"No!" Yomi cut him off. "You're not going alone."

"There's no way we are ditching you." Sipho threw his arm round Thabo.

"You would literally be lost without us," Naledi added. "What sort of friends would that make us?"

"Plus we are treasure hunters," Yomi added and then everyone looked at Kayode.

Kayode sighed. "I guess I knew what I signed up for."

"Thank you so much!" Thabo seemed overwhelmed.

It was at that moment the outpost woman returned.

"How do you know so much about the S.B.L.?" Yomi questioned her.

"I am an outpost master and I've been watching this world for a long time. There are many Igwe outposts all over Africa, and let me tell you a secret: the outposts know everything and we know it first.

We know more than the League and the Guild put together." Yomi had more questions but the woman had moved on, scanning each item. "I need to see your S.B.L. membership cards."

Each member of the treasure hunters handed over their cards for the woman to look over. Kayode and Yomi were the last to have their items approved.

"Kayode and Olorunyomi Adesina." She said their names slowly before handing the cards back. Her eyes hovered over them, examining their faces. "Are you related to Adetutu Adesina?" she enquired.

"She's our grandma!" Kayode nearly bellowed.

"How do you know her?" Yomi asked.

The woman spoke on. "Let's just say Adetutu is not unknown here. Her adventures with the Nkara are legendary." She handed over the last item. "This dedication for Nkara clearly runs in the Adesina family. The outposts are all watching to see what will happen next."

CHAPTER 8
THE CRYSTAL CAVES

The sun continued to bully the treasure hunters with its intense heat as they made their way to Richtersveld. They were still in the thick of the desert, where halfmens trees rose like giants to watch over the land. Yomi had learned from Uncle Olu that the locals called them elephant trunks because of their stems.

The desert was a force of its own but on their newly acquired power bikes, the Vilha Treasure Hunters were up to the challenge.

As Yomi rode through the sands she looked up and spotted a swarm of Zigos flying way overhead, their scorching colour spreading through the sky like streaks of silver fire.

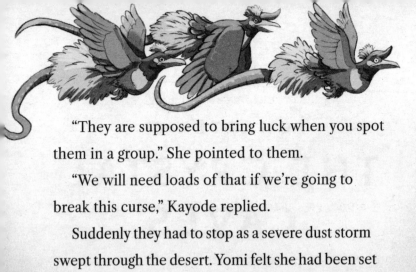

"They are supposed to bring luck when you spot them in a group." She pointed to them.

"We will need loads of that if we're going to break this curse," Kayode replied.

Suddenly they had to stop as a severe dust storm swept through the desert. Yomi felt she had been set adrift in a cyclone of chaos as the ground at her feet shifted and spun madly around her. It even lifted her up a few times and she only just managed to remain on the ground. Sand battered against the group as if trying to separate them from one another.

"Guys, put on your masks and goggles," she shouted into the fog of sand, unable to see anyone. "Kay, stay next to me."

"Always!" Kayode said back.

"Sipho, use the orb." Yomi thought quickly. "Everyone get to the light. We need to stay together and wait for the storm to pass."

The orb shone bright, cutting through the sand blizzard dancing around them. They regrouped, got off their bikes and left them carefully by a tree. Then Thabo released a loose sheet from his backpack, which was big enough for them all to gather underneath and wait for the sandstorm to end.

Yet the storm refused to pass. The dust continued to surround them. As time went by, Yomi knew it was not going to die down any time soon.

"We are never going to make it at this rate," Thabo groaned.

Yomi could tell he was getting frustrated. They had to do something quickly or they would become lost in the sand.

"We need a new plan." Yomi turned to Naledi.

"Can we find a place to wait out the storm?" The heat along with the raging sand blizzard was unbearable.

In response to her question, Naledi pulled out the map from her backpack and examined it for the hundredth time since they started this adventure. Then she put the map away and told everyone to follow her, leading them back out into the world of swirling sand.

Moving slowly and holding each other's hands, the treasure hunters formed a human snake to brave the sand-driven hurricanes, which continued to try to sweep them away.

"Hold on tight to the person next to you," Yomi urged as they powered through the storm to reach cooler grounds.

After nearly being blasted by sand grains again and again and again, and nearly separated, the group found the entrance to a mining tunnel inside a tiny, rocky cavity. Once they had dusted off the sand and drunk some water, Naledi pointed them to a single narrow passageway broken into a rock at a slanted angle.

"What is that?" Sipho questioned.

"An abandoned underground tunnel system that was used by the Tlou mining group years ago," she explained. "The tunnel comes up close to Grootslang's lair, and not too far from Vilha."

The group gathered around the small hole, looking inside.

"Echo!" Sipho sang into the void and his voice spilled deeper into the cave before returning to them. Yomi threw a loose piece of rock inside and heard it crack almost immediately.

"OK, it's not that deep," Thabo said. He pulled the silver tube containing the expanding rope from his back and thrusted the tube into the rock where it embedded itself automatically. He pressed the side button and a thick rope shot out into the dark.

Everybody clipped themselves to the rope using the harnesses they'd collected from the Helix.

"It's pretty dark," Kayode said anxiously.

"It shouldn't be too bad. I've got you," Yomi told him.

He gave her a weak smile. "I know, and I'll get through this because you're here with me."

Yomi shared a fist bump with him. "Thanks, Kay. I'll jump down first."

"No, I should go first," Thabo insisted. "I'm the leader. I need to protect everyone."

"No." Yomi pushed back on this. "You need to stay up here with the others, I should go first."

"I don't want you to be down there and run into trouble alone," Thabo argued back.

"My grandma told me once that a great leader sometimes has to lead from behind and not always from the front," Yomi said and she could see Thabo slowly taking in those words.

He stepped back reluctantly, allowing Yomi to go in front.

Yomi moved to the foot of the hole. "See you all in a few minutes." She remembered her training and took a deep, extended breath. Then she lowered herself using the rope, down into the darkness, where shadows swallowed her whole.

"Thabo was right, it's not that deep." Yomi

pressed her feet into the ground to make sure it was stable. She looked around to examine her surroundings and to check if there were any other obstacles to be careful of. "Come down, guys, but watch out for the spikes," she shouted up.

Kayode was the first one down, keen to rejoin his sister. "Whoa!" he exclaimed when he looked around.

"I know!" Yomi had never seen such formations before. Extra-pointy stalactites stuck out from the ceiling like sharpened ends of swords. Along the ground, there were smaller, rounded stalagmites coming from below.

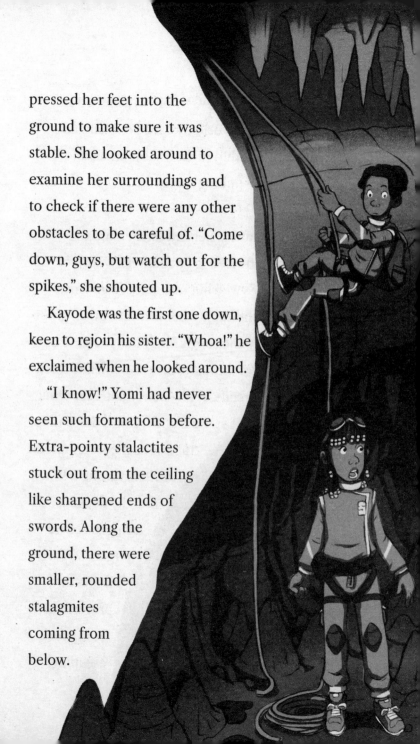

Wanting more visibility, Yomi switched on her new goggles and the world around her changed colour. She switched to night-vision mode and laughed at Kayode pulling funny faces right in front of her.

The treasure hunters headed further into the caves and were surprised to encounter a web. Not an ordinary spider's web but one made from vines. They tangled around each other in a network of green knots and were dry and tough. They had to figure out a way to get through these difficult and thick threads. With each strand scratching at them and trying to keep them trapped as they attempted to climb through. It was as if the dryness was trying to secure its grip on their clothes and prevent them from ever escaping.

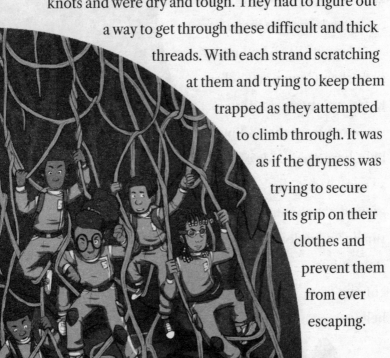

"Stick to the gaps," Naledi offered. "We can probably squeeze through them and pull each other through."

They followed her plan, lifting each other through the tight spaces and scrambling through the holes in the spiralling web. Kayode led the way, helping Yomi, Thabo and the others to crawl through one extremely small crack. Everybody copied Kay's flexible moves as they followed after him to make it safely to the other side.

"I bet no one has been here in years," Naledi guessed as Sipho took a photo of the green webbing.

"But why is it here?" Sipho asked.

"The miners probably set it up to stop other people getting into the mines," Thabo theorized.

They kept going and were making good progress until it suddenly became hard to move. Yomi looked down and could just make out that the floor was covered in a dark brown oozing liquid.

"It's so oily," Kayode commented.

"And gassy!" Naledi added when a large fume of

vapour broke out from the ground.

Soon the treasure hunters were stuck, their shoes fastened in place by the brown substance.

"What if it gets in my hair!" Kayode moaned.

"You can cut it, Kay," Thabo replied as he tried to pull his foot free.

"I will kick anyone who comes near my hair with scissors or clippers!" Kayode shouted.

Yomi tried to soothe the spooked crew. "Everyone stay cal—"

"Oh no!" Sipho cried as Naledi fell forward, both of her legs and one arm trapped in the substance. Naledi started panicking and was on the verge of tears as the glue seemed to harden on her clothes. Yomi could have sworn it looked like she was sinking as well.

Yomi tried not to give in to the terror she was feeling as the glue-like trap seemed to tighten its hold over them. "Please, Naledi, don't move and everyone else stay still." She scanned all around them looking for a way to break free, but it was Sipho who spoke up.

"Thabo, the spear," he said. Thabo pulled it out of his bag, looking confused.

"Thrust it into the ground over there and we can use it to pull ourselves free," Sipho instructed.

"Got it," Thabo said, before forcing the sharp end into a safe patch of ground. Once it was in place, he extended the stick to its full length so it reached all of the treasure hunters.

"Everybody grab it and pull yourself towards the other side." They did as Sipho ordered, hauling themselves to safety. It was especially hard for Naledi but with encouragement, she managed to release herself.

They collapsed on the hard rock, exhausted and wiping off the remaining goo. Yomi breathed out in relief before smiling hard as Kayode complained some of the substance *had* found its way into his hair, with Thabo and Sipho helping him to get it out.

"That was a great idea, Sipho," Kayode praised him.

"Being around Yomi has helped me think on my feet a little quicker," he said.

"We make a great team!" Yomi grinned at them all. "We are in this together."

They continued cautiously through the caves, spotting fossils and some remaining mineral deposits. And even more wondrously there were Nkara!

Yomi immediately recognized many Grand Nkara. She spotted a group of Segrus, thin giant worms with one singular eye that hung on an antenna, crawling along the walls. Wrebbles with their shelled bodies and tentacle-like arms had found shelter in the holes of the caves. A colony of Zicco, tiny ghoulish-green creatures with six legs, emitted a glow that rivalled light bulbs. Luckily, all these Nkara were harmless to humans.

Flashes went off as Sipho captured everything on camera. "The rest of the League are going to be so impressed," he exclaimed.

"Why do you like taking photos?" Kayode asked.

Yomi thought it was a good question – Sipho's camera was like an extra arm.

"Because a picture can scream a million words." Sipho held up his camera like it was treasure. "My grandma says everything can be seen in a photo. The past, present and future."

Sipho used the zoom to focus on a section ahead of them. Once he had taken the photo, he froze like a statue before stepping back and double-checking the camera to make sure he wasn't seeing things.

"No way!" he shouted.

"Don't shout, you might freak out the Nkara in here," Yomi told him.

"Sorry ... but..." Sipho barged past them in the direction he had caught on camera.

"Where are you going?" Naledi called, before they all followed him into a larger crevasse. They gasped as they saw what Sipho had spotted.

Kayode rubbed his eyes. "Are you seeing what I am seeing?"

"Oh yes," Thabo answered.

Deep underground, the group had found a luxurious hoard of the most exquisite gems Yomi had ever seen in her life. Diamonds, rubies and emeralds were everywhere, with sparkling stones embedded in the cave walls.

"You said these mining tunnels were abandoned, right?" Yomi asked.

"Yes, they were," Naledi answered.

"Do we know why exactly?" Yomi was quickly realizing it might not have been humans who had put those booby traps in place. Looking around, she realized the others had come to the same conclusion. Thabo's face was tight as if trying to hold back his emotions, Sipho started to panic, and Naledi and Kayode exchanged worried glances. Given the gems in front of them, she was starting to get a good idea of who *had* set the traps...

As the treasure hunters realized they had accidentally entered Grootslang's cave, the shock blew each of them away. But now they were in the danger zone and had to be on guard.

"The S.B.L. records didn't mention that her cave extended so far," Naledi was stuttering in shock. "I can't believe we're here. In Grootslang's lair!"

Sipho cautiously took a photo of their new surroundings as if scared they would bite.

Kayode was starting to shudder, whispering to the treasure hunters about how Grootslang would swallow them whole if they weren't careful.

Moving together as one, they paced deeper into the cavern, which was piled high with treasures. Despite the dread that now walked with them, Yomi was in complete awe of their surroundings. They all were. She spotted Kayode using a light blue sapphire as a mirror to fix his hair.

"Stay focused, everyone," Thabo urged. "Look out for the Tusk Diamond."

The crew started searching among the loose gems that littered the floor. Some were huge, some tiny. All stunning, all priceless but none of them were the diamond they sought.

"It will take days, even weeks to look through all of this," Yomi said.

"We'll find it – we have to," Thabo said.

The group continued their search before moving into another section to explore there.

Yomi shivered in the chilly wind that crept through the caves. "Guys, do you feel that?" she asked.

Before anyone could answer, a strange sound beat them to it. It was a cutting hiss mixed with the brutal roar of an elephant, and it was racing through the tunnels towards the group. The Nkara around them scattered into their hiding holes.

Everyone knew what was happening but Kayode voiced their fear. "It's Grootslang," he howled.

"Run!" Yomi hurried everyone out of the room. She dared to throw a look back behind her and saw the gems reflecting the snake scales, showing a million Grootslangs.

The treasure hunters were running madly through the tunnels. Yomi couldn't see the Sacred

Nkara properly, but her angry growls chased them through the cave system.

"Any ideas?" Sipho shouted at the group.

"Yeah, I've got one," Kayode shouted back. "Keep running and don't get eaten!"

They came to a fork in the path.

"Which way?" Kayode asked.

"There's more light coming from that one." Thabo made the choice and they all followed him down the left passage but quickly realized their mistake.

"We should have gone the other way." Yomi reflected the peak of terror which now washed over them. A mountain of glittering jewels lay in front of them, filling the back wall of the cave. They were at a dead end.

CHAPTER 9
BEHOLD GROOTSLANG

A prolonged hiss hooked itself into Yomi's heart and went so deep she thought it had stopped beating. She wasn't sure it was working again until Grootslang finally slid into view.

"Wenza ntoni emqolombeni wam?" she hissed to them in Xhosa, but no one answered. They were too busy taking in the creature in front of them.

Grootslang's skin was an electric blue colour, her head exactly like that of a mega-sized elephant. She had long, curled white tusks and sharp black horns, but it was her eyes that stole the breath from Yomi's throat. They were like giant blood-red rubies glittering in the dark, and took Yomi back to the Nkara's rampage at their camp.

"Speak, children, or be devoured! What are you doing in my caves?" Grootslang repeated in English.

Yomi had lost her words while Kayode nearly shivered out of his skin! Yomi darted her eyes around the gem-encrusted room looking for an escape and realized the only way out was back the way they had come, behind Grootslang.

"Great Grootslang, we are sorry to disturb you. My name is Yomi and we are from the Sacred Beast League." She hoped to show how sorry they were.

"How polite, a meal has never said sorry to me beforehand."

"Please can you not eat us," Kayode chimed in.

"You have freely trespassed on to my land. Face the consequences."

Yomi took a deep breath before talking. "We have come for the Tusk Diamond..."

Grootslang shook her head as if expecting this. "You bore me already, like so many before you." She flicked her forked tongue at them. "I wish to eat you now."

"No, you don't need to do that." Kayode grabbed Yomi's arm and pulled her towards the exit, gesturing everyone to follow. "We will leave. It was lovely meeting you..."

Grootslang swung her giant tail to block the exit, her scaled rear missing them by centimetres. Together, Yomi and Kayode looked up at the face of the Sacred Nkara who loomed her head closer to them. "You are not leaving."

Gasps of horror from the group filled the cave. Yomi looked around, hoping to find another exit she might have missed, no matter how small. There had to be one...

Thabo stepped forward. "Do you have any idea what you did when you came to Vilha? Even after my grandfather apologized and begged you not to destroy his home." While Thabo spoke, Yomi gestured with her hands behind her back for Naledi and Sipho to go around while they kept Grootslang talking.

"The stupid boy who dared to break into my lair." Yomi could see the memory flickered in Grootslang's eyes. "You are kin to Letang," she rumbled.

Thabo nodded.

"I should have known. You look exactly like him. You humans are all the same, stealing things, destroying everything in your path."

"We have come to make peace," Yomi urged. "And end this curse which has caused so much pain." While she spoke, Yomi noticed Naledi and Sipho finally slip out of the bejewelled cave.

As Grootslang spoke about the trouble humans

had brought to her over the centuries, including how selfish they were, the Sacred Nkara turned her head, revealing the skin underneath it, where she had been slashed by a sharp sword.

Beast Hunters, Yomi thought. No wonder Grootslang disliked humans and wanted nothing to do with them.

"Vilha will never be free of the curse. There can be no peace between Nkara and humans."

Grootslang narrowed her dark eyes at Thabo, clearly aggravated by his presence. She bent her head closer to him. "You in particular, young one, are very rude to come to my home and ask for *anything*."

"My name is Thabo," he said as Grootslang growled at him. "You never let my grandfather explain things to you. He only stole from you all those years ago because his mother was really sick," Thabo revealed, his eyes about to flood with tears. "He didn't think you would notice a few missing gems to help pay for some of her hospital bills. He only did it for her."

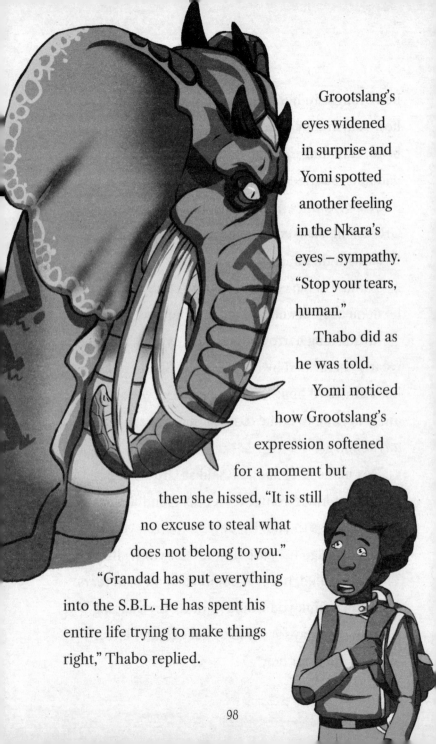

Grootslang's eyes widened in surprise and Yomi spotted another feeling in the Nkara's eyes – sympathy. "Stop your tears, human."

Thabo did as he was told.

Yomi noticed how Grootslang's expression softened for a moment but then she hissed, "It is still no excuse to steal what does not belong to you."

"Grandad has put everything into the S.B.L. He has spent his entire life trying to make things right," Thabo replied.

"That is good to hear, however it is far too late for Letang to make amends to me. Other Nkara may feel differently but I do not. You humans have entered my space and must now pay the price."

At that point Grootslang looked around the room and noticed she was a few meals short.

Yomi braced herself, whispering to Kayode and Thabo to prepare themselves for an attack.

"You have been abandoned by your friends," Grootslang taunted, coiling her large body into striking stance. Yomi, Kayode and Thabo also got into position. And when the Nkara lunged for them, the trio leaped out of the way before circling back on her, making sure to face her. They had learned the art after dodging the Roklens!

Repeatedly, Grootslang rumbled and hissed as she swung for each of them in turn, but the three were able to use their smaller size against the Ancient Nkara and she kept missing them.

As she whipped her tail towards the exit, Grootslang grinned. "You cannot dodge me forever. Prepare for your end."

CHAPTER 10

THE GREAT TRADE

A showdown with a Nkara was always to be avoided but this time, Yomi didn't have much of a choice. Grootslang's eyes lingered on them as she prepared to strike again. *What is she thinking?* Yomi wondered. Was she truly not moved at all by why President Letang did what he did? To enter the caves of the most feared Nkara in the world, he clearly had been desperate.

Grootslang reared her great head backwards like a cobra, ready to swing for them once more.

Thabo pulled out the spear-like weapon. "Get behind me!" he instructed Yomi and Kayode as he prepared to face off against Grootslang.

"What are you doing?" Yomi said to Thabo, not

sure if he was the bravest person on the planet or the most stupid.

"It's like he wants to get eaten!" Kayode complained.

"I am impressed you dare to challenge me." Grootslang looked down at Thabo with a mixture of amusement and seriousness.

"Wait!" Yomi held her hands in the air, trying to think of a way to solve this. How could they convince the Sacred Nkara? Then a small glimmer of an idea popped into her head. "How about a trade?" She fished into Kayode's pocket and pulled out the pyronite.

"That's mine!" Yomi elbowed Kayode in his side. "Sorry," he grumbled.

"What is it?" Grootslang bent her head towards Yomi to examine it.

"It's pyronite." Yomi could see the redness of the mineral reflecting in the beast's eyes – their shades were almost identical.

While Grootslang examined the mineral mere centimetres from Yomi, she was able to get an even closer look at one of the oldest Nkara in the world. Her blue scales radiated with colour, except for one, which shone brightly with a white light.

And Yomi realized it wasn't a snake scale – it was a diamond. She nearly gasped. The Tusk Diamond was part of Grootslang's skin!

It looked as though it was attached loosely and Yomi hoped it would easily come off with a gentle tug. She knew she would have to wait for the perfect moment.

She looked back up at Grootslang. The Nkara was bedazzled by the mineral. She stuck out her forked tongue to wrap around it, but Yomi snatched it away in time.

"You can have the pyronite in exchange for all of us leaving the caves safely," she stated.

"Fine," Grootslang huffed and fully moved her tail to unblock the exit of the cavern. "You may join your friends and leave and I will skip my meal – just this once."

"Great negotiation, Yomi," Kayode huffed with relief.

Grootslang dropped her head to roll her tongue over the pyronite but Yomi was not finished. "And the Tusk Diamond."

"Then no." Grootslang blocked the opening once again.

"No!" Kayode echoed, falling to his knees as freedom was snatched right from their grasp.

"I want us to part as friends, if that's possible. With the curse on Vilha broken and with humans and Nkara one step closer to peace," Yomi said. Her words clearly stunned Grootslang. It was more than a trade – it was a sign of possible reconciliation.

Grootslang shook her mighty head. "I think not.

You ask too much," she hissed at Yomi before she suddenly charged.

"Yomi!" Kayode and Thabo shouted, but Yomi had anticipated this.

Grootslang swung her heavy head, her tongue sticking out like a rope to seize the pyronite. Yomi dodged it, throwing the gem high into the air along with a few other red stones she'd picked up earlier. She juggled them before throwing them to the far edge of the room. Grootslang sprang after them.

"Run!" Yomi yelled.

Her mind went into overdrive as she and the others sprinted away from the dead-end cave, not sure which way to go to lose Grootslang in the tunnels.

"I can't believe you threw away my pyronite," Kayode said.

"I didn't." Yomi held it up, then gave him and Thabo a quick flash of something else before quickly stuffing it in her pocket.

Thabo couldn't believe his eyes. "The Tusk Diamond! How did you do it?"

It had all happened so quickly. Yomi had slipped it free from Grootslang's skin before the Ancient Nkara had sprung after the fake pyronite. She had removed it so softly that Grootslang hadn't even noticed, but she would very, very soon.

"Grootslang is going to be *so* angry!" Kayode whined.

The trio ran through the caves, lost and going in circles. In the background, an angry Grootslang howled, realizing she had been tricked twice.

"Are we ever going to see the surface again?" Kayode moaned, just before he banged into someone and fell down.

"Kay!" Sipho helped him up.

"I'm so happy to see you." Naledi clung to Yomi and Thabo as they reassured her they were unharmed. "We've found a way out and made it safe so we can escape FAST."

"We can go now – we've got the Tusk Diamond!" Yomi told them.

Sipho and Naledi looked shocked.

"What's that?" Yomi questioned, looking at the object in Naledi's hands.

Naledi held up a pole made from some broken branches stuck together with glue from the booby trap. "Oh, we made these in case Grootslang came after us."

Sipho held up some more. "We made enough for all of us."

Kayode took one of the longer poles, looking over it with care. "We need to go now before Grootslang finds us."

Right on cue, the Sacred Nkara swarmed into view, her eyes burning with anger as she sped down the crystal corridors towards them. "Give me my pyronite! Give me my diamond!" she yelled at them.

"Go! Go! Go!" Yomi grabbed Kayode's hand.

The group ran together down the passageway with the elephant-serpent drawing closer.

This time, as they approached the thick oils bubbling on the floor, they were ready. Naledi and Sipho had worked quickly while the others had been talking to Grootslang. They had thrown several stone rocks on to the glue trap, which Naledi, Sipho and Thabo used to cross the oil safely. But by the time all three had stepped on them, the stones had disappeared into the glue, leaving Yomi and Kayode stranded on the other side.

Yomi looked all around, hoping there was another way to cross. Their friends were starting to panic from the other side.

With Grootslang close behind them, Yomi and Kayode stood before the glue trap. Kayode, who was still holding the long pole Sipho had created for them, planted it deep into the glue trap. "Yomi, follow my lead." He held firmly on to the pole and Yomi copied him. Grabbing it tight, she was confident that together they could do anything.

As Grootslang turned the final corner, the pair did a small run up and with all of their combined strength, used the pole embedded in the floor to vault off the ground.

The pole bent slightly, the momentum and power swinging them forward away from Grootslang. Together, Yomi and Kayode flew above the glue trap

and landed on the other side where Naledi, Thabo and Sipho were waiting.

Grootslang realized too late what was happening as her entire body landed in the greasy glue. The group watched as the Nkara struggled to break free. She tried to slice through the substance, but the more she moved the more it stuck to her scales, got on her horns, tusks and even her trunk.

The Sacred Nkara turned her blood-red eyes on the Vilha Treasure Hunters. "Curse you, humans, curse you all!"

CHAPTER 11

PROMISES AND CURSES

Despite making it to safety with the diamond, Yomi didn't like to see Grootslang stuck in the glue. Even if she had threatened to eat them!

"Mission successful!" Sipho commented, patting Thabo on the back who looked on at a struggling Grootslang, his face unreadable.

"Time to go?" Naledi offered.

"Yes ... but we can't leave her like this," Thabo said softly, still unable to take his eyes off Grootslang.

Yomi pulled out the pyronite again in response, knowing deep in her heart they had to save the Nkara.

Grootslang was becoming more than annoyed as

she tried to wriggle free of the glue, which had now settled all over her scales.

"We will free you from the glue trap and give you the pyronite but you have to promise we can leave the caves, and the curse will definitely be broken when we take the Tusk Diamond back to Vilha," Yomi stated.

"No, I would rather stay like this," Grootslang replied.

The group all looked around at each other, unsure what to do next. Yomi was surprised Grootslang would still not budge from her thinking, despite being completely trapped and having no way to escape on her own.

"Can we make a new agreement? What do *you* want Grootslang?" Yomi asked.

"I desire nothing more than to live the rest of my life in peace. Undisturbed, unbothered. To live knowing what is mine will remain mine."

"Privacy," Yomi proposed.

"Exactly," Grootslang confirmed.

"I will tell the S.B.L. They will create a new protective zone for you, which will include these caves. Now we know where they are. No one will bother you again," Yomi promised. "We will also help you get out of the glue and give you the pyronite. For this, we want our freedom, the Tusk Diamond and for you to end the curse on Vilha."

Grootslang thought for a while before she finally answered. "I accept your trade."

"Thank you, you will not regret it," Yomi said.

While negotiations were taking place, Sipho and Naledi had hastily made some lassos out of vines. They threw them around Grootslang, then the treasure hunters pulled on the firm green cables, freeing Grootslang.

Once safely out of the trap, the Sacred Nkara shook herself free of the vines and excess glue which stuck to her.

"Why would you choose to help me?" Grootslang asked.

"Because these choices are important. They can change everything," Yomi answered. "They can change people's lives, cities, countries, even the world." She thought of how President Letang's choice to come to the cave had consequences that had affected everything and everyone for years afterwards. "And I choose a future where humans and Nkara are *both* protected. All are safe."

Yomi stepped forward to hand over the pyronite.

Grootslang stared at the gem before looking back at them. "All of you may jump on me." She wiggled her snake-like body. "I shall guide you out of the caves."

After a stunned silence, Yomi replied. "Since you offered, sure!" She climbed the scales first, which were unexpectedly warm. Then she remembered that while snakes were cold-blooded, elephants weren't.

Yomi's acceptance prompted everyone else to join. Kayode wrapped his arms around her as everyone else grabbed the person in front of them and held on tight as Grootslang slid her way through the caves, swaying her head from side to side. Grootslang took them back out of the caves, heading into the cooler hours of the desert.

Rocks and
botterboom trees were embedded
into the rugged terrain of the Richtersveld,
intertwined with long stretches of sand.
She slid across the ground, moving stealthily until they
reached the edges of Vilha then came to a stop. "This
is as far as I will take you."

"Thank you for the lift," Yomi called out.

"I am impressed by your craftiness, your bravery
and your choice to free me," she said. "Now the
agreement is in place, I will stay in the safety of my
caves, except for when there is a Yinza moon."

"A Yinza moon?" Sipho looked baffled. Even the
grandson of a Yinza expert hadn't heard of it.

"What is that?" Yomi asked.

"It's when the moon shines brightest because of Yinza magic on its surface and *from deep within*."

"What does a Yinza moon do?" Yomi questioned.

"When I bathe underneath it, I feel stronger. A Yinza moon very rarely appears but it should soon, and when it does, I will be ready to use its power."

"It helps you live longer?" Naledi deduced.

Grootslang nodded. "I have lived many more years than what is to be expected – I'm the last of my kind. When the gods punished me and my brethren, I was confused, upset. Once we were many and then I was alone." Yomi's heart felt heavy at this. "I fled into the Richtersveld and that night there was a Yinza moon. The rays shone brightly on me and all my injuries from the great splitting were healed."

Yomi couldn't believe it. When would the next Yinza Moon appear, and what would it mean for Nkara?

"But I must warn you," Grootslang continued, sharing one last piece of advice with the children. "Not all Nkara are open to new agreements with humans. Especially given the behaviour of Beast Hunters."

"We will be careful but the S.B.L. are different. We believe in One World for All," Yomi affirmed.

Grootslang nodded, accepting her words. "Goodbye." She started to leave but then stopped. "Thabo," Grootslang called out to him. "Tell your grandfather ... tell Letang we are now at peace and there is no more anger on my part."

Thabo bowed his head. "Thank you."

"Once you return the Tusk Diamond to Vilha, the curse will be lifted." And with those parting words, Grootslang slithered back across the sands. The Vilha Treasure Hunters continued to watch her, only the snaps from Sipho's camera breaking the silence.

"Now that is the perfect shot to end this story." The photographer sighed happily.

"Guys, we actually did it!" Kayode celebrated.

High fives swung through the group like a wave.

"We got the diamond back!" Naledi shouted.

"Show it to us again," Sipho said.

Yomi pulled it out of her pocket, and for the first time they could take a proper look at the Tusk Diamond. It was like a curved drop of moonlight;

it outshone the stars and dazzled like the sun.

"It's not quite over yet," Thabo said.

The group looked to where Vilha once stood and headed towards the broken town. Slowly they entered the land and walked among its ruins.

As they walked through Vilha, the Tusk Diamond felt hot in Yomi's hands and it got hotter the deeper they went.

"How do we know if the curse is bro—" Kayode was interrupted by a giant tearing sound followed by a rumble. The group clung to each other as the earth vibrated.

A white mist appeared around them and for a moment the sun was obscured. The only light was now coming from the Tusk Diamond, which jolted in Yomi's hands as she struggled to keep a grip on it.

The ground at her feet was pulsating and then the town's buildings started spouting out of the earth as if being spat back up into the world.

"Whoa!" Kayode shouted as all around them the town started to rebuild itself. Bricks began to reform into houses and other structures like pieces of a jigsaw.

When it was done, the mist disappeared and the Tusk Diamond was no longer hot in Yomi's hands. For a few moments, disbelief hung over them. None of them could believe what had just happened before their very eyes.

"We actually broke the curse!" Naledi shouted.

"Thank you," Thabo said to everyone before turning to Yomi. "Thank you."

"Your grandad will be so pleased," Sipho commented.

"He can finally come home." Thabo gently took the diamond from Yomi. "It's ... perfect."

"It's fantastic," Kayode added as Sipho took a photo of it.

"This is history," Naledi concluded.

The diamond glowed like a piece of moon rock in Thabo's hand.

"Time to get back to Vioolsdrif – let's hope the adults are still there," Sipho said.

"They're going to be delighted when they see we've broken the curse and we show them the diamond!" Yomi exclaimed.

"I hope they're not too angry that we've been gone so long..." Thabo replied.

"We should start planning our excuses," Naledi suggested.

"Anyone got any good ideas?" Kayode prompted.

But no one did – they had used them all up!

While the group tried to figure out what to tell the adults, Yomi could still feel the diamond's lingering warmth in the tips of her fingers. Grootslang's words about the Yinza moon flashed back in her mind. Yinza was an even bigger force than she imagined. She didn't have all the details yet but she would soon, and she would use it to protect Grootslang and all other Nkara.

CHAPTER 12
RESTORATION

The fresh breeze from the Orange River brushed over Yomi as they approached Vioolsdrif and the S.B.L. members waiting for them.

Yomi and Kayode sprinted towards Uncle Olu, who looked ecstatic to see them. Yomi and Kayode jumped on him, knocking all three of them to the floor.

"I'm so happy to see you both." Olu hugged them tightly.

Naledi's father lifted her high into the air while Onalenna squeezed Sipho tightly before telling him off in a quick sway of Tswana.

"Uncle, you won't believe what happened," Yomi started. "We went down the river, we paddled the whole night and ended up in Namibia."

"You crossed the border," Olu said slowly.

"Then we went to a place called Stinger's End, which looks abandoned but is actually home to Roklens." Kayode took over the story.

"Roklens!" Onalenna turned to Sipho. "You got involved with Roklens!"

"I took some photos," Sipho told his grandma. She looked pleased.

"We have been searching the whole region for you guys. After the camp was abandoned, we tried not to fear the worst. We knew you had gone downriver to lose Grootslang but we lost your trail," Olu explained.

"Once you got to Namibia, why didn't you turn around once you knew you had lost Grootslang?" Onalenna questioned.

"We went to the Helix," Sipho answered.

"I navigated us there," Naledi explained.

"I'm proud of you." Naledi's dad put his arm around her.

"There you are!" another voice broke the conversation.

"Grandad," Thabo exclaimed. "What are you doing here?"

"I was informed that the younger members of our expedition were unaccounted for and there were supplies missing from our stores. All of you, present yourself for a debrief," President Letang demanded.

Yomi followed her fellow treasure hunters to stand in front of the president. He gave them all a once-over before his eyes landed fully on his grandson. "Thabo, you are the oldest. What happened? Why didn't you come straight back?"

"It's not his fault..." Yomi spoke up but Olu made a sign she was not to get involved in this conversation between grandfather and grandson.

"Why did you put yourself and your fellow League members in danger?" Letang asked.

Thabo didn't answer, he simply handed over the Tusk Diamond.

Letang looked shocked at the offering – his jaw nearly fell off his face!

"My dearest Thabo, what have you done?" Letang stared at his grandson before looking at the others. "What have you all done?" Gasps broke out around them when he held up the diamond.

"I can't believe it." Olu put his hand over his mouth.

"Letang, are you OK?" Onalenna asked.

"I... I..." The president looked on the verge of tears. "I never thought I would see it again."

"We did it for you, for Vilha, for the S.B.L.," Thabo explained, pulling Yomi forward. "It was Yomi who really saved the day."

"We made a deal with Grootslang – she wants her territory to be protected." Yomi passed on the Ancient Nkara's request.

"Whatever she has asked for shall be granted. She has returned this and mended a fifty-year mistake," President Letang said.

"She said all is forgiven between you and her," Thabo relayed.

"She did?" Letang said softly. "I'm so pleased but I have a million questions."

"So do I," Olu inserted.

"Me too!" Onalenna added.

"The real question is – are we in trouble?" Kayode spoke up.

"I believe..." Letang pulled Thabo into a hug. "You can all be forgiven."

To bring life back to a once ruined village would take courage and much more. It took community, teamwork and unity. The S.B.L. were prepared to bring about this vision, a new Vilha.

However, before the work began, President Letang sent out requests for surviving relatives of Vilha to return to the remains of the town for a special ceremony – to celebrate the end of the curse and the return of the Tusk Diamond to its rightful home.

Yomi knew the day of the Vilha Restoration would go down in history as one of the S.B.L.'s greatest achievements.

Everyone invited had assembled in an area in the town centre. Here the Tusk Diamond had been placed on a plinth for all to see. Yomi noticed many older people weeping as President Letang started speaking.

"This is a new start for the people of Vilha, an achievement for us all. I know our parents, grandparents and ancestors are all smiling down on us. A new motion is to be passed to establish new borders for Grootslang," Letang announced to those who had gathered. Young and old, everyone was connected to Vilha. "Today is a day that no one thought possible. The Tusk Diamond has come home because of these young people." He nodded to Yomi and the treasure hunters in the front row. "They are the future of the League and the key to peace between Nkara and humans everywhere."

Once Letang finished speaking, the next part of the celebration began. Dancers appeared and took over the courtyard to perform the Setapa. The routine was filled with tapping feet, constant clapping, raw singing and powerful movement. All the dancers wore traditional outfits made from animal skins and shells, and their costumes swung from side to side. A story of joy and triumph was being told through dance.

After a few songs, the dancers encouraged others to join them. Yomi watched as Thabo dragged his family members to step into sway with the dancers. Soon after this, Sipho and Naledi dragged their families on to the floor. Before Yomi knew it, most of the S.B.L. members were joining in on the traditional celebration, which was danced all over Southern Africa.

Kayode quickly picked up all of the moves and was dancing alongside the professionals in no time at all.

Yomi was enjoying watching the dancing, until Uncle Olu said he needed to speak with Yomi and Kayode privately.

With Yomi's help, he eventually managed to drag Kayode off the dance floor. "You two have done a good thing for the people of Vilha and for Grootslang," Uncle Olu said, the music still booming in the near distance. "I'm very proud of you both."

"I'm proud of us too." Yomi hugged Kayode, bringing him close.

Uncle Olu smiled at them. "Now the Tusk

Diamond has been returned to its rightful place, we must keep it safe. After all, it is of Yinza origin and others may come looking for it."

Yomi knew he meant the Beast Hunters. "The S.B.L. will keep it safe," she vowed.

Yomi thought about the work that lay ahead but one thing kept pushing to the front of her mind. "The woman at the Helix said something to us," she told Uncle Olu.

"Yeah, she knew grandma's full name," Kayode remembered.

"Grandma is an S.B.L. member," Uncle Olu replied. "How do you think your dad and I got into all of this?"

"I thought so," Yomi replied. It explained her grandma's deep knowledge of Nkara.

"And she isn't just an S.B.L. member," Olu added. "She founded the S.B.L."

"Really!" Yomi shouted. She had so many questions! When was that? What led to its creation?

"Olu! Where are you?" someone called out in their direction.

"Chuma! Over here," Olu replied to the young man, before muttering to Yomi and Kay, "He should be in Cape Town. I wonder what he's doing here?"

The man ran over to them and bent down, panting.

"Long time no see." Olu clapped the man's back. "Catch your breath."

"There's no time to catch my breath," Chuma answered. "There has been an emergency call from the Congo Basin."

"The Congo! Who sent it?" Olu asked.

"Daba Toure. He said he needed help immediately."

"Uncle Daba needs our help?" Yomi said. They had met Uncle Olu's close friend and fellow senior League member in The Gambia.

"What's going on over there?" Olu asked.

"Missing Nkara from the basin," Chuma explained.

"That sounds like a mystery." Yomi was already keen to head to the Congo to find out what was going on.

"I thought we could finally have an *actual* holiday..." Kayode breathed. His dream summer plans were changing faster than he could keep up with.

Yomi grabbed Uncle Olu's and Kayode's hands. "We're going to the Congo!"

**JOIN YOMI AND
KAY ON THEIR NEXT
ADVENTURE IN**

COMING SOON

"A monstrously fun adventure" Louie Stowell, author of LOKI

YOMI AND THE FURY OF NINKI NANKA

DAVINA TIJANI

ILLUSTRATED BY ADAM DOUGLAS-BAGLEY

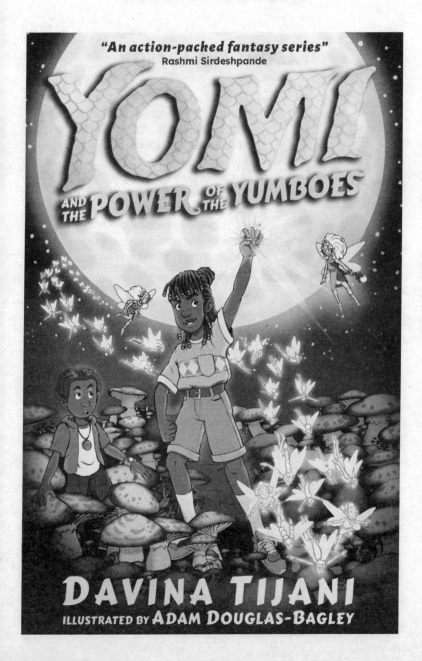

"An action-packed fantasy series"
Rashmi Sirdeshpande

YOMI
AND THE POWER OF THE YUMBOES

DAVINA TIJANI
ILLUSTRATED BY ADAM DOUGLAS-BAGLEY

ABOUT THE AUTHOR

Davina Tijani writes speculative and fantastical stories for both adults and children. She was born in London and holds degrees from University of East Anglia and University College London. She grew up on Star Wars and other science fiction, fantasy and horror films and stories. She is a huge lover of mythology and enjoys incorporating it into her writing.

𝕏 @davinatijani

ABOUT THE ILLUSTRATOR

Adam Douglas-Bagley is an illustrator and storyteller from South London. Ever since he first picked up a pencil Adam has had a passion for illustrating fantastical worlds and filling them with stories. With his illustrations, Adam endeavours to explore the transportive and timeless ability of storytelling to enthral audiences. He hopes to inspire anyone with a story to tell, to pick up a pencil and share their own worlds for others to traverse.

📷 @adougiebagofdrawings